TUGBOATS

Henry Holt and Company, Inc.
Publishers since 1866
115 West 18th Street
New York, New York 10011

Henry Holt is a registered
trademark of Henry Holt and Company, Inc.

Published in Canada by Fitzhenry & Whiteside Ltd.,
195 Allstate Parkway, Markham, Ontario L3R 4T8.

Library of Congress Cataloging-in-Publication Data
Maass, Robert.
  Tugboats / Robert Maass.
  Summary: Describes the different kinds of tugboats and the work
they do, various parts of a tugboat, from its wheelhouse to its
engine room, and the jobs of the crew members.
  1. Tugboats—Juvenile literature. [1. Tugboats.] I. Title.
VM464.M32 1996   387.2'32—dc20   96-17884

ISBN 0-8050-3116-2
First Edition—1997
Printed in the United States of America on acid-free paper.∞
10 9 8 7 6 5 4 3 2 1

ROBERT MAASS

TUGBOATS

HENRY HOLT AND COMPANY · NEW YORK

Tugboats are the best-known and best-loved workboats of the water. Their strength, size, and ability to turn quickly help them to push and pull vessels of all sizes in, out, and around the waterways.

No two tugs are exactly alike. Each one is unique, like the people who work on them—the captain, the engineers, the mates, and the deckhands. You won't meet a crew member who could imagine working anywhere else.

Tugboats come in all shapes and sizes. They are built for the type of job they perform. Some are made for pulling a load; others are made for pushing. Little shipyard tugs move small loads around the harbor, while large oceanworthy tugs carry big loads across the sea. There are tugs that can push 500-foot-long fuel barges and other tugs designed for salvage-and-rescue operations.

Barges of great length and weight are pushed through the nation's waterways by special tugs called towboats. Despite their name, these tugs don't tow but rather push their loads.

Tugs haul all kinds of things, from gravel to garbage, wheat to wood chips. They'll pick up a barge, take it to be loaded, and push it somewhere else.

When a big ship slides into a crowded dock, at least one tug must be there to help. When that same ship pulls out again, a tug or two are needed to pull it into clear water.

A big cargo ship is ready to leave its berth, to cross the ocean. Tugs arrive to pull it out. No time is wasted. The ship's thick towing line—called the head line—is tied to the tug's front (the bow). The tug smoothly backs the vessel away from the loading dock and pivots on the head line to push alongside the bigger vessel. When the ship reaches deeper water, it can sail on by itself.

Most ports require that a tug-boat be used to bring ships in, since the tug captains know the local waterways best. The job is often done with the help of a harbor or docking pilot. He is a specially trained tug captain whose job is to go on board the big ships and direct the tugs. He is like a musical conductor, coordinating one or more tugs to safely bring ships in or take them out.

Many tasks that tugboats perform are routine, but there is always the possibility of surprise. Putting a load of barges 600 feet long into a lock is a precise job that takes great skill and teamwork. A lock is a holding area with gates that open and close. The water level is raised or lowered to allow boats to pass through. The pilot, who may not be able to see the front of his load, is guided into the tight-fitting lock by his mate, who speaks to him on a walkie-talkie.

But what happens if there's a fifty-mile-an-hour crosswind as a tall, empty barge enters that same tight squeeze? That'll get any pilot's heart racing until the big load is safely in the lock. The crew must always expect the unexpected. Nature can quickly turn an everyday job into a dangerous challenge.

In the winter, many bodies of water freeze. The only way ships can gain passage is with the help of ice-breaking tugboats, which are run by the Coast Guard. These boats have special hulls (bottoms) that are designed to break ice up to thirty inches thick. The tugs slide on top of the ice, and their weight crushes the frozen water. These special tugs clear paths for other tugs, and help boats that get stuck. When the temperatures are really low, ice-breaking tugboats will work every day to keep the channels open for shipping.

Tugboats are controlled from the wheelhouse, also called the pilothouse. It's easy to find the wheelhouse because it's always on the top of the boat and full of windows. A pilot moves all around the wheelhouse to see as best he can. While operating the tug, he'll even step out on the wheelhouse deck to see how close he is to a ship or dock.

The wheelhouse is full of gauges, screens, and equipment. There are compasses, depth finders, and other navigational tools like maps and charts, as well as engine and steering indicators. Also in the wheelhouse are controls for a powerful searchlight and a loud horn. A tug pilot always keeps a logbook for writing down everything the tugboat does.

The most important controls are for steering and power. Most tugs have two propellers—called screws—that operate separately or together. The pilot can steer the boat with this power system. If one screw is pushing harder than the other, the boat turns.

A pilot needs radar for many reasons. Radar shows every object and vessel on the water for miles around. It's most useful at night, especially when there's fog and it's hard to see. If a pilot didn't have radar, he might bump his load into another vessel or a pile of rocks.

A tug captain communicates with a radio. The captain talks to the crew as they throw lines to and catch lines from boats and barges. The captain is also in contact with other boats on the water. Most of the time the captains talk about work, but they often talk to each other like friends do on the phone. Today most tugs also have cellular telephones.

While the pilot steers the boat, the engineer makes sure that the engines and other mechanical parts of the tug are working well. It's a never-ending job of checking oil levels and temperatures, watching pressure gauges, greasing, cleaning, and replacing worn or broken parts. Tugs work very hard, so their moving parts need to be watched closely for wear and tear.

A tugboat is usually surrounded by rubber bumpers made from old truck tires. They're either hung over the sides of the boat or cut up, sandwiched together, and attached to the sides. Since a tug is always sidling up to other vessels, the bumpers provide protection for both the tug and whatever it's touching.

The mate and the deckhands take care of the day-to-day maintenance of the boat. They secure lines and cables while the tug is working. Rain or shine, they're out on deck getting the job done. When there's spare time, ropes need to be spliced and checked for fraying. Deckhands often take turns cooking, though anyone on board is welcome to prepare a meal. When a crew spends so much time away from home, a good meal becomes pretty important.

Many tug crews work two weeks straight on the boat and then get two weeks off. For the weeks on duty the crew become a team, together twenty-four hours a day. If the crew is big enough, the hands work in shifts—six hours on and six hours off—around the clock. If the crew is small, the hands work whenever necessary and as long as it takes to get the job done. Since shipmates live so close together and for such long periods, it's important that they get along well. A crew is like a family.

An experienced crew and a fast-moving, powerful tugboat work together to keep the waterways safe. But no matter how routine the daily tasks, there is always the risk of danger. That's the challenge of life on a tugboat. As many crew members would agree, it's more than just a job—it's a calling.